KING GRUMPYGUTS

by Stan Cullimore

Illustrated by Peter Kavanagh

There once was a grumpy King. His name was King Grumpyguts, and he never smiled or laughed.

Not smiling

Not laughing

I don't know why he's so grumpy. He's got an enormous palace and the finest gardens that money can buy.

2

ven more things

Gold plated
motorbike

Diamonds on
his rollerskates

In fact, King Grumpyguts
had everything.
Well, everything but one.
He didn't have happiness.
He was not a happy king.

All day, the people in the palace searched for King Grumpyguts.

Not here

Or here

Not here either

But he was nowhere to be found.

15

As for King Grumpyguts, he stayed in the small house with the little wooden door, happily ever after, and spent the rest of his days sweeping up and growing roses.

KING GRUMPYGUTS and the Pirate

One windy day in autumn, King Grumpyguts put down his cup of tea and looked out of the window ...

The truth is, I'm bored. What shall we do, Bob?

We could always go to the park.

I know, let's go to the park.

That's what I said.

24

So while King Grumpyguts and the pirate looked for treasure ...

Bob looked for his bone.

They dug,

and dug,

and dug.

44

So now, whenever King Grumpyguts looks at his vegetable patch – he laughs and he remembers his friend the pirate and the treasure. The treasure that the pirate's great-great-great-grandfather forgot to bury.

Where did I put that key?

The End